This
Treasure Cove Story
belongs to

_____

THE BIG BOOK OF PAW PATROL

A CENTUM BOOK 978-1-912396-94-8
Published in Great Britain by Centum Books Ltd.
This edition published 2019.

1 3 5 7 9 10 8 6 4 2

Centum Books Ltd, 20 Devon Square, Newton Abbot,
Devon, TQ12 2HR, UK.

www.centumbooksltd.co.uk | books@centumbooksltd.co.uk
CENTUM BOOKS Limited Reg.No. 07641486.

A CIP catalogue record for this book is available
from the British Library.

Printed in China.

centum

nickelodeon

A Treasure Cove Story

THE BIG BOOK OF PAW PATROL

By
Mary Tillworth

Whenever there's trouble in Adventure Bay, the PAW Patrol will save the day! They're six tough pups with special jobs and talents who are always ready to race to the rescue with their super-cool vehicles and tools.

When Ryder calls, the PAW Patrol reports to the
Lookout to get their rescue mission. No job is too
big and no pup is too small!

CHASE

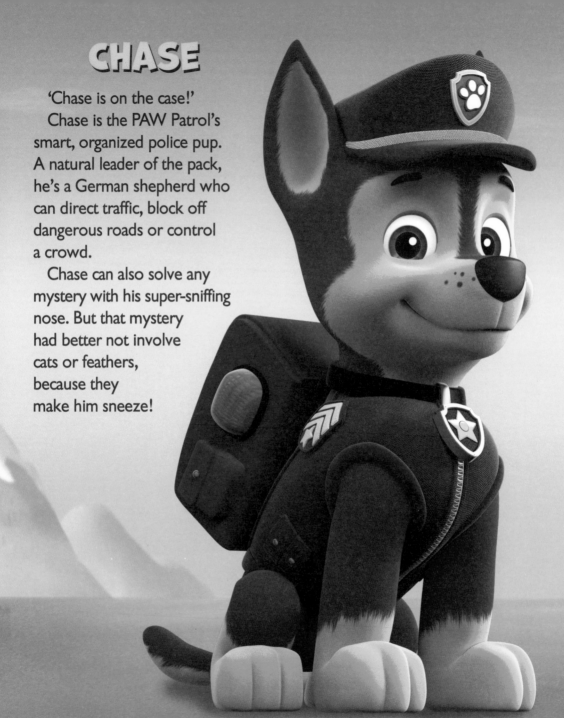

'Chase is on the case!'
Chase is the PAW Patrol's smart, organized police pup. A natural leader of the pack, he's a German shepherd who can direct traffic, block off dangerous roads or control a crowd.

Chase can also solve any mystery with his super-sniffing nose. But that mystery had better not involve cats or feathers, because they make him sneeze!

Chase's Pup House transforms into a police truck. In his Pup Pack are a megaphone, a searchlight, a net and other things to help this police pup keep the peace.

MARSHALL

'I'm all fired up!'
Marshall is the PAW Patrol's
fire dog. He's a Dalmatian
who's always ready
to race to the rescue
– though his excitement
often makes him
a little clumsy.
When running into
the Lookout for a mission,
he'll trip over his own
feet, and even knock
over the other pups!

But no matter what
happens, Marshall always
lets his friends know
that he's okay!

Marshall's Pup House turns into a fire truck. His Pup Pack holds a double-spray fire hose that helps him extinguish all kinds of trouble.

RUBBLE

'Let's dig it!'

Rubble is the team's construction pup. He's a tough Bulldog who loves to build, dig and get dirty. But he also loves warm baths at Katie's Pet Parlour.

Rubble is great at skateboarding and snowboarding. He also has a soft spot for 'itty-bitty' kitties and other cute critters.

Rubble's Pup House turns into a digger with a bucket shovel and a drill. His Pup Pack opens into a bucket arm scoop so he can dig into any situation.

SKYE

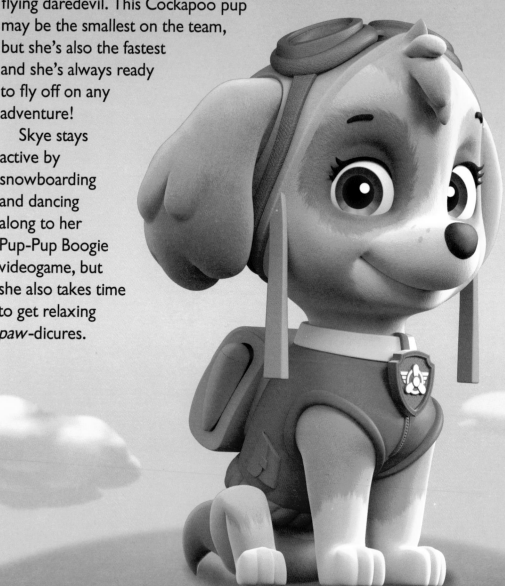

'This pup's gotta fly!'

Skye is the PAW Patrol's fearless, flying daredevil. This Cockapoo pup may be the smallest on the team, but she's also the fastest and she's always ready to fly off on any adventure!

Skye stays active by snowboarding and dancing along to her Pup-Pup Boogie videogame, but she also takes time to get relaxing *paw*-dicures.

Skye's Pup House transforms into a helicopter.
Her Pup Pack has wings that pop out to help
her fly into action.

ROCKY

'Rocky to the rescue!'
Rocky is the recycling pup
on the PAW Patrol. This
mixed breed is one
creative canine. He has
a thousand ideas and
can often turn someone
else's trash into his treasure.
His motto is 'Don't lose
it – reuse it!'

Rocky can get a little
scruffy because he's not
a fan of baths. In fact,
he doesn't ever like
to get wet!

Rocky's Pup House transforms into a recycling truck. His Pup Pack includes many different tools and an awesome mechanical claw.

ZUMA

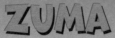

'Ready to dive in!'

Zuma is the team's water-rescue dog, a fun-loving Labrador and the youngest member of the PAW Patrol team. He's happy and energetic and is always trying to get the more serious pups to lighten up.

Zuma loves the beach and anything water-related. This playful pup surfs, dives and even enjoys bath time!

Zuma's Pup House turns into a hovercraft.
His Pup Pack holds air tanks and propellers
to help him dive deep underwater.

RYDER

Ryder is a ten-year-old boy who runs the Lookout and leads the PAW Patrol. He adopted and trained each of the puppies to be a part of one terrific team.

When someone needs help, Ryder calls the pups, picks the right ones for the job and rolls out with them! And when the work is done, he makes sure they all get a well-deserved pup treat.

THE LOOKOUT

The Lookout is home and headquarters to the PAW Patrol. When Ryder gets a distress call, he calls the pups, who gear up during the lift ride, get their mission at the top floor and then slide down into their Pup Houses, which transform into vehicles. Then they roll out to save the day!

At the top of the Lookout, the PAW Patrol watches
over the whole city and responds to any calls for help.
The pups gather for their mission here and Ryder
organizes the pack and decides which pup is best
for the job.

PAW PATROL BADGES

CHASE

MARSHALL

RUBBLE

Each member of the PAW Patrol has a special badge showing what they do and how they protect the citizens of Adventure Bay.

Whenever there's an emergency, the
PAW Patrol pups line up for duty. The members
of this smart, disciplined team rely on their
own unique skills – and each other – to get
the job done right.

After they've completed a mission, Ryder and the pups
enjoy playing in the Pup Park at the base of the Lookout.
No matter how big the adventure, the PAW Patrol always
has time for a game, a laugh and an ear scratch from Ryder.
    The citizens of Adventure Bay are in good paws with the
PAW Patrol!

Treasure Cove Stories

Book list may be subject to change.